Clover

Morning is a time for decision, for momentum, for enthusiasm;
a time that restores to man the freshness of his will;
a departure; the start of a journey.

— Gabrielle Roy

To my Mother and to Mother Nature, who always gave me comfort and protection.
— N.R.

To Nadine.
— Q.L.

Clover

Text copyright © 2022 Nadine Robert
Illustration copyright © 2022 Qin Leng
Copyright © Milky Way Picture Books

Translation by Nick Frost and Catherine Ostiguy
Book design by Jolin Masson

The artwork for this book was created with ink and watercolor.

This edition published in 2022 by Milky Way Picture Books,
an imprint of Comme des géants inc. Varennes, Quebec, Canada.

Library and Archives Canada Cataloguing in Publication

Title: Clover / Nadine Robert; illustrations, Qin Leng;
translation, Catherine Ostiguy, Nick Frost.
Other titles: Trèfle. English.
Names: Robert, Nadine, author. | Leng, Qin, illustrator. |
Ostiguy, Catherine, translator. | Frost, Nick, translator.
Description: Translation of: Trèfle.
Identifiers: Canadiana 20220001634 | ISBN 9781990252143 (hardcover)
Classification: LCC PS8635.O2235 T7413 2022 | DDC jC843/.6—dc23

ISBN: 978-1-990252-14-3

Printed and bound in China

Milky Way Picture Books
38 Sainte-Anne Street
Varennes, Qc J3X 1R5
Canada

www.milkywaypicturebooks.com

story by

Nadine Robert

art by

Qin Leng

Clover

translated from French by
Nick Frost and Catherine Ostiguy

Milky Way
Picture Books

In a beautiful clearing,
nestled among mountains
and forests, lived Clover.

The child was the youngest member
of a big family that lived on a small farm.

It was home to almost as many goats
as Clover had brothers and sisters.

That morning, the sky was clear
and the house was bustling.

Morning, Iris!
Hello, Peony!

"Let's go pick some blueberries,"
said the eldest child.

"How about we go to
the river to find some
mussels instead,"
suggested another.

*I would much
rather pick
mushrooms!*

Clover wanted to do all of these things,
but couldn't choose just one.

This was often the case.

So the child stood frozen on the doorstep,
unsure of what to do next.

Come on, Clover!
Let's go mushroom picking!

Clover did want to go mushroom picking,
but, for some reason, couldn't take the first step.

*What's the
matter, Clover?
Don't you want
to come with us?*

"It's not that," the little one replied.
"I simply can't decide what I want to do."

I like picking mushrooms...

... but I also like finding mussels in the river because I get to see frogs.

"Then go to the river!
There are no wrong answers, Clover.
You'll be fine either way.
You can always pick mushrooms another time.
But don't let others decide for you."

"Hmm," the child whispered, still uncertain.

As Clover was deep in thought,
the frogs' joyous singing came to mind.

I've decided!
I'm going to the river!

"All right!" replied
Clover's brother.
"We'll go together!"

And off they set,
walking happily
along the path to the river.

The river was
calm and the children
knew the best spots to look
for mussels.

With their feet
in the water,
they lifted each mussel
one by one and put
them in a large bucket.

Nearby, a delighted
Clover was petting
some friendly frogs.

Suddenly, something caught
Clover's attention over in the ferns.

First, there was a rustle,
then a little cry.
Curious, the little one stepped out
of the water and into the thicket.

A young goat stuck out its head from between two ferns.

Peony! What are you doing here? Did you follow us?

Clover took a step toward the animal,
but the little goat pranced away.

Wait!
Get back here!
You can't be in
the forest by yourself.
You're too far from the farm.
Peony! Come back!

The young goat was faster than the child. It quickly disappeared behind some rocks.

Clover started running after it.

As Clover got deeper and deeper into the forest, fear started to creep in.

"If I walk too far, I could get lost,"
thought the little one.

I should find
my way back
to the river...

... but I can't
leave Peony alone
in the forest!

Once again, Clover didn't know what to do.

Clover turned to face a big, tall oak
that stood a few steps away.
"Great Oak, I need your help. Should I keep
looking for Peony or walk back to the river where
my brothers and sisters are waiting?"

Clover's little arms stretched out
to embrace the tree. The child
pressed an ear against the bark.

You can talk to me.
I'm listening.

The bark smelled good, but the tree didn't
utter a word — not a single piece of advice.

Disappointed, Clover let go of the oak.

Although the tree hadn't given a clear answer,
Clover found its presence calming.

*I must
find Peony!*

The child took a deep breath
to gather some courage.

Clover walked deeper into the thicket,
calling out the goat's name.

Peeeeeony!
Where are you?
Come back!
I have to take
you home.

Suddenly, the child looked down
and saw animal tracks on the ground.
Clover followed them to a fork in the path.

*Some of the tracks
go to the left, along
the stream...*

*... and others go to
the right, deeper
into the forest.*

Clover was unsure: Were the markings
those of Peony's little hooves?
The child didn't know which path to follow.

The little one walked toward the stream.

"Gentle Stream, I need your help.
I don't know if I should follow
the path to the left or to the right."

Clover laid down next
to the stream, leaning
over the water.

*You can
talk to me.
I'm listening.*

The stream was crystal clear and its music was soothing.
But it didn't utter a word — not a single piece of advice.

Clover thought for a moment.

Although the stream hadn't
given a clear answer, Clover found
its soft whisper reassuring.
The child took another deep breath.

I'll follow the path to
the right, the one that
goes into the forest.
Peony probably
went that way!

But before Clover could set off again,
a tiny, shivering ball of feathers at the bottom
of a tree caught the child's attention.

"Poor little bird! What happened to you?"
Clover looked up and saw a nest resting
on the branch of a tall poplar.

Oh! I see.
You fell from
your nest.

The child wondered if it was wise to climb the tree
and put the bird back in its nest. Would it be better
to bring it home and nurse it back to health?
Or to not touch it at all and keep looking for Peony?

The little one looked up to the poplar and
heard the rustling of wind in its leaves.

"Oh, Wind! I need your help. I don't know
what to do with this bird... And Peony?
What will happen to Peony?"

Hesitant, Clover laid down
on the grass.

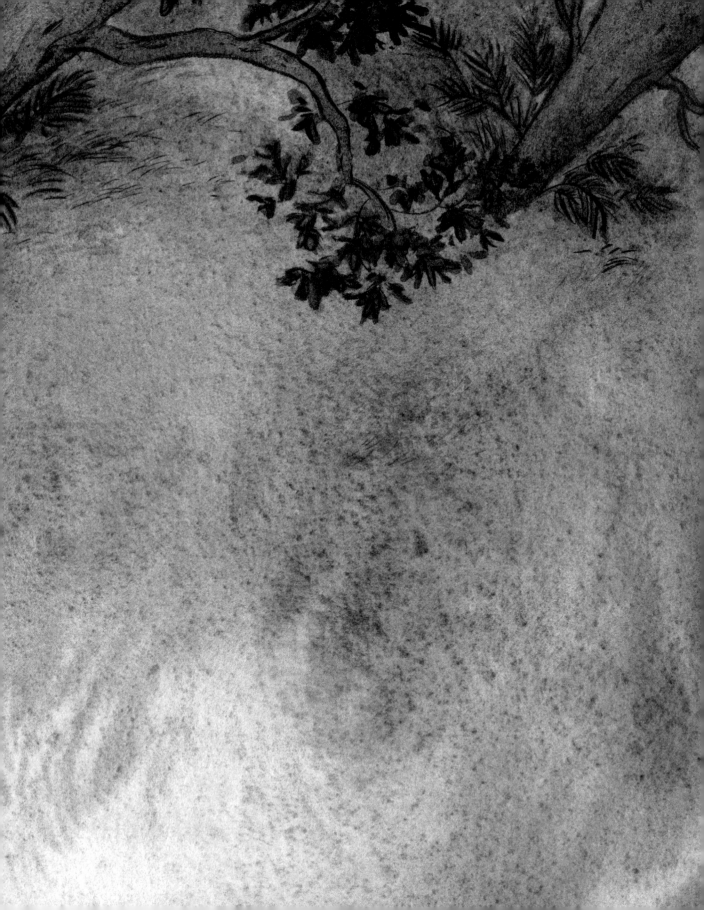

The wind blew gently against the child's face.
But it didn't utter a word — not a single piece of advice.

Clover looked up at the leaves that
were dancing softly in the breeze.

Although the wind hadn't given a clear
answer, its gentle blow was inspiring.
A little voice inside led Clover to the bird.

Surely, it would be eaten by a fox or
a weasel if it remained on the ground.

Clover lifted the bird gently.
"I'll keep you safe in my bonnet."
And together, they bravely
began climbing the tree.

Don't be scared.
You'll soon be back
in your nest.

Then,
I'll go and look
for Peony.

Carefully placing the bird
back into its nest, Clover
suddenly heard the faintest
noise carried by the wind.

This time, it was very real.
In the evening breeze,
the child could hear whispers.

There were some familiar voices...
and the soft tinkling of a bell.

In the growing darkness, the child saw lanterns moving through the forest, swaying from side to side at the end of tall sticks. A luminous procession of brothers and sisters was roaming the woods, looking for Clover.

And it was led by none other than Peony.

All the way up on the poplar's branch,
Clover yelled out:

*Peeeeeony! Peony!
You've found
your way!*

"And we've found you," said Clover's
brother, looking up at the branch.

*You gave us
quite a scare!*

The children had found Peony wandering
alone in the forest. They decided
to keep walking along the path,
thinking Clover must not be far.

Turns out,
they were right.

Listening when our heart speaks
will always lead us where we need to go.